# A HOUSE FOR LITTLE RED

Modern Curriculum Press
BEGINNING TO READ Series

# A House for Little Red

Margaret Hillert

illustrated by
Kelly Oechsli

MODERN CURRICULUM PRESS
Cleveland • Toronto

Library of Congress Catalog Card Number: 79-85953

ISBN 0-8136-5513-7 (paperback)
ISBN 0-8136-5013-5 (hardbound)

9 10 02 01 00 99

Here, Red.

Here, Red.

Come here, Little Red.

Come here to me, Little Red.

Run, run, run.

Here is a cookie for you.

I want to play.

We can run and jump.

One, two, three.

Here we go.

Here is something.
Here is a blue ball.
Jump up, Little Red.
Jump up, jump up.

Go, Red, go.

Go and find the ball.

Oh look, Red.

Look here.

Here is something for a house.

I can make a house for you.

Go in, Red.

Go into the house.

Oh, oh.
It is not a house.
You look funny.

Here is a yellow house.

Go in here.

Go in, go in.

Oh my, oh my.

The house is down.

It is not for you.

Come, Little Red.
Come and look.
We can find a house.

Here is a little house.
I see something in it.
One, two, three little ones.
It is not for you, Red.

Look up, look up.

I see a house up here.

Oh, my.

It is not for you.

Look here, Red.
Look down here.
Here is a little house.
See the mother.
You can not go in here.

Come, Red.
Come away.
It is not for you.

Oh, here is Father.
Father is big.
Father can help.

Father, Father.

Can you make a house?

Can you make a house for Little Red?

I can. I can.
Come and see.
I can work.
You can help me.

Down, Red, down.

You can not work.

You can not help.

Go away.

Oh, Father.

The house is big.

Where is Red?

Come, Red.

Go into the house.

Red is in the house.

A big house.

A blue house.

A house for Little Red.

**Margaret Hillert,** author of several books in the MCP Beginning-To-Read Series, is a writer, poet, and teacher.

## A House for Little Red

A boy finds a house for his dog with his father's help, told in 49 pre-primer words.

### Word List

7 here
red
come
little
8 to
me
run
is
a
cookie
for
you
9 I
want
play
we
can
and
jump
one (s)
two
three
go
10 something
blue
ball
up
11 find
the
12 oh
look
house
make
13 in
into
14 it
not
funny
15 yellow
16 my
down
18 see
20 mother
21 away
22 father
big
24 work
help
27 where